KNOB

for Young

KNOB

Russell Helms

Contents

Death is hard,

candy. Most animals eat the placenta. She lost thirty pounds on a diet of tendons and ligaments. Goddamn you is not a suggestion. The hydrogen bomb is difficult to conceal in pastry. If you can't get rid of the tapeworm, at least try to work with him. There is no such thing as a good tongue lashing. The sickness unto death is fairly obvious. The smog over Los Angeles, is, in fact, a blessing from God.

Decaffeinated tea is a poor substitute for liquid nitrogen. Murder, on trains, is to be expected. When preparing ape, discard the feet and hands. The virus has many secrets but tells no lies. The Lord may be my shepherd, but I still want a new computer.

The waddling yellow parrot seemed distracted by the eclipse. After the high-speed train derailed, several bystanders were heard to mutter. Vanilla pudding goes with just about anything. Twelve times a minute, five minutes go by. Those people are waving at the airplane. Hard yellow pimples and drool complete the package and the epileptic boy was friendly but unreliable and retired steel workers fidget with bagels and the time of death was determined to coincide with the moment of decapitation and many years ago biscuits were never frozen. It would be nice if I knew better.

Loud cursing neither distracts nor agitates the venomous cobra. The brain is inherently moist. After losing several games, the hockey team abandoned their glue sticks. Marooned, eating cherries. The tapeworm is not standard. The divine medium: Jesus was a C-student.

Cough drops prevent cough drops. I joined a gang of locusts, but failed to stomach their ideas. A box inside a box is not a box. The triangles in my brain annoy the squares. In a distant galaxy, there is no milk, only milk powder. I can see over the next mountain because it is behind me. Never cross your eyes when approaching the speed of light. The blood made her teeth seem whiter.

In the town of Scissors there is no hair, no paper, only stones. Lick my yellow teeth. Oligarchy on toast. I am surrounded by skin. A candle cannot wax. The eye of the bass is upon you. Hurricane Catatonia left a wake of silence. The rat lives in the sewer by choice, begging the question of poverty. Picking peaches with one leg. Broken monkeys, more bananas. Crabs on my scabs. Swollen ankles for breakfast. Mules nodding in Tennessee.

No matter how hard I chewed, the gum remained the same. Seraphim or succubae? Eating apples in a coal mine. On becoming a grain of sand, I no longer saw the sky. A penny saved never says thank you. Strawberries and bream.

I blew out the candle then blew out my brains—I am lighting the candle. The mall in Rome, Georgia, wasn't built in a day. Into the mail Strom Thurmond fell. Perhaps one day when we stand in line for air there will be less television.

A harelip can, in fact, reach Cuba. Candlesticks of gold lead to murder. I have yet to want

to strike a child and kick a dog instead. Far out
is best out. Amway products. My skin is alive
with hair! The horny priest ravaged his bishop-
ric. Bare not false teeth against thy neighbor.
Crucified with Tourette syndrome. In order to
be unglued, first, one must come unglued.

Wow and Zowie have a cat, Ethelbert. Dru
keeps his social skills in a brown paper bag.
The bag is very small, as big as an apple. Un-
employment rates are low and that's okay as
long as there's room for me. My head belongs to
many people. Most of them wear black and gray,
except for the one in a coma who wears a thin
white gown. It's a crazy world said the psychia-
trist orbiting the earth in a yellow canoe.

I use a tiny German torque wrench to tight-
en the screws in my glasses. I peeled a yield
sign and ate the flesh hesitantly. If you feel my
pain, why should I bother? Eating Vienna sau-
sage with a cold sore. Blister pudding with salt.
The Bobbsey twins are more interesting than
Stephen Dedalus. A hardboiled egg between
bites of dry toast. A dizzying array of antiemet-
ics. It really wasn't Guy Fawkes day was it?

In Wisconsin, the act of having one's photo
taken is viewed as tiresome. Few cars have glove
boxes large enough to accommodate an adult
sperm whale. My glasses are tinted, frosted,
shatterproof, and scratch resistant, but I still
can't find them. In the land before time, watches
were worn primarily as jewelry. If you can count
the holes in your head, count yourself lucky.
If you build a better mousetrap, the mice will
complain. Within the confines of a major seizure

disorder, froth and spittle seem quite ordinary.
Snap!

the sound of a leg breaking. A tissue is
useless against slugs and cow's tongues. All I
need to know I learned from the rattlesnake at
the zoo. A pod of peas and a pod of whales are
dissimilar. The flash camera exists briefly. The
paper man is never safe. After the house fell in, I
learned to read. After my watch stopped, I found
a tick on my leg. If you lose a battle with cancer,
what has the cancer won? Vomiting on a severe
burn makes things worse. It's disturbing when
the cracks in the wall get smaller.

Never swallow a woodpecker. Pesto sauce
is not a cure for gonorrhea. Just between you
and me, the laws of the universe are a bit harsh.
God's man-breasts make him seem like a woman. You can wipe your ass with iceberg lettuce.
She kept her father's head in a hope chest. The
frankness of the matter and the furter of the
beans yielded better buns. The stiff hair felt at
home in the black mole. It's useless to speculate
on the origin of the unicycle. If pancakes are
round why don't they taste round? I put white
paint on the wall.

It's embarrassing to drown in an inch of
water. My camelhair sweater is never thirsty. If
I defecate on your head after I stab you twelve
times, it could be that I don't like you. Never
wash your face with red ants.

If the mole weighs more than a pound, it's
probably not a mole. The common housefly
deserves better. Raw sewage and raw cabbage
are dissimilar. People, who talk in elevators, are

likely to kill you. Never whip the wrong baby. Papier-mâché scrotum. Which is worse, parachute failure or paradigm shift? Wrinkled egg yolk. Driving under the influence of Persian rugs. The spermatic cord is not a toy. Helen Keller was curious. The spotted owl and spotted underwear are dissimilar. Grenade launchers are harmless. A bird in the hand is unsanitary.

Starvation and diarrhea are not complementary. The oyster makes its own sauce. What if you were a pixel, then what? Cat hair does not cure pink eye. Warm sockeye. After a deadly riot, tea is nice.

The gadfly knew all about the wallflower. The gargling grizzly bear presents little danger. Self-similarity seems vaguely familiar. Once fried, green tomatoes are useful for eating. The party to end all parties will be a sad affair. According to the quadriplegic, the spineless man seemed a bit arrogant. Curly hairs in the sink may explain the yellowed toothbrush.

To lessen the shock, "genital warts" is preferable to "genital gristles." The neurosurgeon rarely said "whoops," but when he did it was with feeling. The part in her hair was played by the wind. In the country, urban legends are true. Incest is hard to swallow.

I cannot tell you how relieved I was when told that the object in my rectum was indeed smaller than a breadbox. Strangulated hernia with gravy. Bad jobs: lightning greaser, enema repair, god killer. A license to kill is proof enough. I brush my teeth with tartar sauce. All my friends have a history of cold sores.

People dehydrate me. Mass murder saves
time. Hangnail with a paper cut and a side of
fries. German picnic: specific gravity of the
potato salad clearly marked. The meek shall
inherit the bottom of my shoe. A minor poet
has many dead canaries. Diamonds hidden in a
bowl of cold milk. Blessed are the peacemakers
for they make possible the next war. At the first
signs of yeast, the posse turned back. Politics,
religion, crosswalks.

The piss poor are shit out of luck. Don't take
any wooden nipples. An ounce of honorable
mention is worth a pound of manure. In hind-
sight, I miss my foreskin. The Protestant work
ethic includes the productive cough. The terra-
cotta sandwich exists. Bee's wax is not a kind of
mayonnaise. Jesus really liked the little children. Smelling vomit, I drove hurriedly past the
bread factory. The cords in Ray's neck matched
his pants. The woman delivered a pizza shaped
like a baby. It's really about how far the train
drags you.

A grove of angry almond trees. Don't be
Captain Curt with me. Chicken soup for the
crack whore. As long as the vassal ate, the vassal
was not lean. Instead of Calgon, smash your penis between two bricks. The trick is to taste your
tongue as you swallow it. The literal arts journal
published very little fiction. My delving license
expired. Relying on the dead to bury the dead
requires a plan B. I didn't actually spill my seed.
The harelipped queer liked mapplethorpe on
his pancakes. The coffee mug typically is wrinkled with yellow teeth. Weebles wobble is suffi-

cient. Many people crowd the sidewalk. I drive
with one hand on the horn, in case my dead
brother should appear. Throwing out stacks of
unread paper. There were blankets hanging in
the elevator. There is a New York Bagel shop in
Birmingham.

A razor is sharper than scissors and fits easily into your pocket. That purple cat food bag
is half full. Men with thin lines stretching from
their cheekbones to their ears work in banks.
Being of the clan, I naturally lusted for my sister. A trembling chihuahua cowered in the desk
drawer. The paper towels seemed to disappear.
Grandmother coughs weakly while clutching
a tissue. The pitter patter of rain frightens me.
There is a spy who cuts meat at the grocery
store who knows my name. The splinter in my
heart pricks with each contraction. The hob-
bits at church prefer to sit in the aisles. More
powdered sugar on that donut please. Really
small books have their place. The generic cough
syrup came with a small plastic cup. Pardon my
French said the prisoner. Please God, let the
ketchup be red.

The hymen lick maneuver requires practice.
At the Language Games, John took the bronze
in epithet hurling. It's the stranger's ear wax that
smells bad. Little boy laughing in Liechtenstein.
Trading secrets at the flea market. At the funeral
home, corpses are kept at room temperature.
Diploma: paper or plastic?

Freckles of stale cat litter. The rich are better
able to afford steel plates in their heads. I can't
find my placement test. A strawberry-blonde

vomiting chocolate ice cream. The amputee's nub seemed angry. The accidental hanging requires a rope or its equivalent. The executioner rarely beat his wife.

Subatomic beard particles. Drastic measures include the fecal ounce. The subtle appeal of mayonnaise and bacon. Never hesitate to inquire about murderous tendencies. Just because a rat's intestine looks like spaghetti doesn't mean that it is. Driver. The pardon is given with a quiet smile. Just playing around, Todd impaled his sister. Grandfather coughs with hope. One big toe more attractive than the other.

A zipper pecks noisily inside the hot dryer. Her neck hurts while clutching a load of clean clothes. Wearing leather shoes without socks. The blue tee shirt, folded, lying on the chest of drawers. I don't have a camera, so I use my friend's. During the siege of Stalingrad, many insults were exchanged. The field pea does not enhance playing surfaces. An encyclopedia of war contains many lies.

I read the obituaries with pictures. The small town riddled with flu, rattled with phlegm. The hopeful yellow of new earth moving equipment. Tiny numbers on extension cords and tampon sleeves. The boiled egg has met its fate. Driving without a license is feasible if you don't have one. Waiting to be fed, three cats hold their tails erect. The people of Poland laugh when told that their country has disappeared three times.

"My bowels is just like water" may be construed as a cry for help. Over time, the process of dying becomes monotonous.

The fireplace is

fake. Reading by the light of a peanut at the South Pole. The test of time is necessarily a lengthy process. The painting covered the wall. A mat of hair molded to the drain slows the flow of milky water into the sewer. The majority of cartoons are not funny. Each year the gavel doubled in size until finally no one could lift it. *Wheel of Fortune* is all about language.

I rarely grasp anything. For several weeks now I've been watching to see if her fingernails really do keep growing. Duck hunters have little else to call themselves. The washer/dryer is a great combination. The funeral home director liked to stand and nod at the passing cars. Talking sex to youngsters is enhanced by the use of prostitutes and cadavers. That style of hat is funny. The entrance to the cave exhaled a stream of cool air and then, ominously, breathed in. Cursing cleanses the palate much as celery. She teased me with her bosom. Stealing welcome mats from the poor. The cold of the meat. Hens scratching and pecking, oblivious to the full moon. Still not interested in parades of any sort. Making eyes at the librarian.

Music piped into the bathroom. The Blessed Virgin in for yet another abortion. In Russia, the snow belongs to the people. Great leaders get that way. Shopping for corpses on a tight budget. Holding the egg too long. Old people arguing about whether or not it rained during the night. The horse with the most spots is sometimes the fastest. Open a door if your house fills with ants. My radial artery is displaced yet provides part of my hand with rich red blood. Realizing that the proof was in the pudding, the detective confiscated the recipe.

The dirty mop water fooled no one. Easter Sunday falls on the same. The collard green when prepared correctly produces a flatus that passes easily at convenient two to three hour intervals. The flatus is not noxious and is considered by some to be a pleasant surprise. Drag hair net spray. Please everyone, settle down. Two page registration form for the bass tournament. The octopus made a poor witness.

The neck of the lying doctor seemed white and greasy. Flu outbreaks follow flu shots. The rental fee for the portable toilet was reasonable, but the deposit was not. The absolute last day to turn them in is Wednesday, October 7. We need each other.

Halloween is just around the corner. Broken shoelace on the driveway. Not everyone in the Luftwaffe enjoyed flying. A little boy with red hair thinks about death. Writing up a storm, it began to rain. My son is not gay. He sat here every night and read this Bible. When I found out, then I knew. Blue suede shoes are scarce. The crackle and swish of grinding pubic hair. Wearing an old suit to a job interview. Furling umbrellas in the desert. Asleep, lactating.

Eyebrow dandruff clings to his lens. At the art gallery opening, complimentary wine and beer made an otherwise unimpressive exhibit seem lively and sophisticated.

Prison tattoos typically mean something. Pink petals encircle the stamen. The average American tourist in Rwanda, when given a choice, prefers the assassination-style bullet-to-the-back-of-the-head over death by hacking. Further study is indicated. As a rule of thumb, donate less than half your blood volume. His writing style was described by *The New York Times* as wooden. Circumcision is boring; genital mutilation isn't.

Friendly fire is a nice way to die. Don't let your guard down just because it says rest area. Pitchfork is not a game. At the art museum, the guard did not touch her gun, yet I knew she wanted to. Mass spectrometry creates jobs. Little black specks in the bottom of the glass. There is always room for one more cat. The gym teacher seemed to favor squat-thrusts. In the land before time, a cup of coffee was ten cents. Parts of me say yes and parts of me say paste. She was a garbage man and now she owns her own business. Mind over manners. Pol Pot is dead. His handwriting seemed to be a font. In order to punch a hole in the ground, one must fall from a great height. More perfect. Games played to the death are not games.

Incest on Sunday

is especially bad. The proud peacock had no idea that his tail feathers would be sold one day at a cat show for fifty cents apiece. As he was about to be baptized, the old man died and went straight to hell.

If a nuclear bomb helps just one person then I think it's worth it. Used hubcaps are more expensive than new ones. Fifteen percent of the time, I tip my hat to the waiter. Smoking crack is prohibited during standardized testing. An excess of tongue. Vinyl siding comes in a variety of vinyl colors. The one-legged man always put his best foot forward. Successfully faking mental illness. Fur is soft but that doesn't make it right.

The numbers just kept getting longer. The colostomy tissue was wet, crimson, and puckered like an everted anus. The marijuana cookie was too sweet and hurt my teeth. At the freak show, the Fat Lady was embarrassed to see a spectator larger than she was.

The crippled children on the bus stared hopefully at the joggers passing by. If your pee seems dark and laden with excess minerals, try running it through one more time. The television was responsible for the divorce, along with the VCR. Wasp stings cure bee stings. Volume has to do with stereos. The pillow seemed a bit fancy, even for a coffin. Eager to draw attention away from her wooden leg, Tina carried a horned toad. Drastic measures include the half cock.

Flying over the steaming volcano, Bob discovered a stiff hair on his nose. I lost the instruction manual and contacted the manufacturer immediately for a replacement. Blessings in disguise are just disguises. God is great, God is good, let us thank God for multiple drownings. Down the hatch to grandmother's submarine we go. His things are in print for about fifteen minutes. Perhaps the best line in the book was the one drawn on the inside cover, perhaps by a child, say seven. The children pointed cruelly at the humpbacked whale. By not learning, you learn something else. In some cultures, a full set of teeth may be construed as dowry.

A flock of Fokkers strafe stray sheep. Bit parts in a small theater. Priceless diamonds should be easy to acquire. Following the brutal beating, the yeast infection only added insult to injury. I was saddened when told of the muon's short lifespan, but encouraged when told that the muon's extreme speed made it seem to live longer. Rimes with geyser. The blistering boil of oatmeal rivals that of grits. Don't let the delicate appearance of the heather fool you. The cattail roots were edible but luckily we had a can of potted meat. To guess the number of jellybeans in a jar, think about how many might be in there.

The buffalo pushed the snow aside with its muzzle only to find a shirt made of hemp, which it ate without ill or weird effects. The funeral confirmed our suspicion. You are a child until you have one. Clueless among clues. We found it in someone's garbage. Fill out information on back of coupons to qualify for future offers. Minimalist music employs a great number of instruments. There were two black hairs, thinner than the rest, growing, it seemed, from the same follicle. Program the universal remote for your particular television and VCR. Remove the tags from your pillows and mail them to Senator Orrin Hatch. It got to the point that no one understood.

On the planet Gonad, cleats are necessary for traction. Real cotton candy is filling. Shriveled umbilical cords and dried okra stems. The dry lakebed yielded few secrets other than those guessed at previously. Could you have cataracts? Why some people should avoid decongestants. Dragging the lake with heavy chains proved useless until Hiram remembered to attach the hooks. It was dark, so she did not notice the yellow film on his tongue.

Jerry's subscription to *National Geographic* expires in May, two months after his scheduled execution. The steam room was cold and dry. The principal text of modern existentialism. Eating parched peanuts with a sore throat. If you are blown from the summit of Mount Everest, you will fall several thousand feet being violently dismembered in the process as you strike various ledges and rocks. Freshly bruised knees. Zig Ziglar meet Dirk Diggler. After douching with a new herbal product, Springtime in Paris, Stephanie felt clean and refreshed yet retained a slight odor of sloughing menses. At the American concentration camp, the children were given Ritalin. I don't want the extended warranty. If you mention it one more time, I'm outta here. While handling snakes at church, two pears dropped from Ida's bra, creating quite a stir. After the doctors went on strike, it seemed as if the people no longer wanted to die. Inside the iron lung, Tim often touched himself in the presence of friends and family. For Christmas, Satan gave his sister's baby a death rattle.

Professional wristwatch wrestling. John the Baptist gave head. The Good Samaritan suddenly recognized the beaten Jew as one of his largest depositors. I combed the book for the part about her hair. Popping zits is one way to express yourself. He dribbled the ball, not the thermometer. In certain parts of the world, "God is good" is funny. The barber's pole. Always pray before eating meat. Cum sodden. In the world of pants, the KKK is sort of the Levis of hate groups. The salesman broke his promise. Most travelers fail to realize that flight departures and arrivals are based on Fibonacci numbers. It was during the aftershocks that Glen bowled a perfect 300.

Dried mayonnaise. Entertain outdoors with our beautiful new garden furniture. Never trade baseball cards in the middle of a stream. I was sure that I had seen that gravy somewhere before. For heroin addicts, grace periods for payment of rent and utilities should exceed six months. In a doctor's office, steal everything you can. As Christ ascended to Heaven, he noticed that the people looked like ants. The blackhead has seen better days. Incontinent on a cool rainy day.

The hardest part about Donna being hit by the train was piecing everything together afterward. Republican or democrat: paper or plastic. In Paris, "It's been awhile since the people rioted" means something. Sewing oats requires patience. The white bread was plain to see. Unless you have a gun, it's difficult to monopolize a seesaw. One rarely uses the plural of penis.

900 pounds

later. There were too many boards in the floor. The influx of whores into the small country town dramatically reduced the incidence of incest there. Pea gravel smarts. The instructions in this section are for touch call phones—phones with a push-button pad, which is called the touch pad. Frank, a disciple of Satan, decided on the candy apple. Not long ago in a place far, far away something happened that will soon not be forgotten. Fish patty.

I remember feeling disturbed upon learning that the sweet amber fluid was not Coca Cola. The train could stop on a dime, but no one would ride it. Drilling kneecaps in Belfast. Larry forgot the Q-tip in his ear and answered the phone. Cutting teeth. Most of the proctologist's patients noticed that the instruments weren't very clean. Lips black with herpes. Unless you watched him make it, don't eat the shepherd's pie. The courtesy flush is a kind of warning. The congressmen got together and donated spare shovels to the struggling zoo. Pulitzer Prize in Poetry means that it will be a good read, perhaps fantastic. The vending machine next to the portable toilet looked new. Take time out to share, discuss, pray, and encourage one another. Seventy dollars worth of self-help books is a kind of creative denial. Wild sex seemed to temporarily relieve Tom's bad back.

At the beach, a paper towel may be described as functionally weak. Each time the

Jehovah's Witness said "Jesus," Margaret rolled her eyes and said "cunt." Always choose crash over crash and burn. Debbie reached down between her legs and tied her shoes. Egg wash.

During a protracted famine, fellatio may save your life. The cause of John's death was high school. Little white egg things on her edible underwear. "No pain, no gain" makes hanging seem more reasonable. A bad tooth is similar to a bad relationship. Such lies! as could only be told by doctors and mechanics. The skull has the consistency of bone. A Filipino, pushing the manila envelope.

Squirming beneath the rubble. Keep this copy for your records. This year's madness made for another year of non-stop soup. Convenient folding capabilities. It was the red dress, the red dress, that, and the red lipstick. Renting the sky is expensive. Squeaky bacon. Pol Pot's poop. Harry, a recent graduate of Wharton, failed to sign his W-2 and consequently went mad. Simicolon policy against can't sir. She preferred her enema way up in the ass. Following a NATO air strike, a rowdy gang of pilots met their wives at Red Lobster. It takes strength, agility, and practice to impale children on bayonets thrown into the air in front of their mothers. A broken nose in the mashed potatoes. Having been in the jungle for six weeks and having lost his rifle, Jonathan lowered his trousers and urinated in the direction of gunfire.

There are dozens of teenagers who would kill themselves for a penny. Hard up for cash and pressed for time, Tom's existence weighed in at thirty-two pounds. A world atlas covers a lot of territory. Think globular, act jocular. At the thrift store "not for resale" doesn't matter. Professor Hamilton's use of the phone book as a text irritated the university bookstore to no end. Mary Todd Lincoln splitting hairs with Abe. The oral surgeon's choppy language frightened his patients. To leave a lasting impression on strangers, shoot them in both knees.

Oswego is a real place with people and everything. Renting a backhoe behind your wife's back. Most slaves were not sold on the idea of freedom.

Apparently I gagged on the silver spoon. This is your receipt. Even if the stewardesses are pretty, never board a burning plane. In the Luftwaffe, kersplat meant something. The geisha had very little patience with the Butoh dancer's advances. After attending public schools for twelve years, Justin found the monkeys at the zoo highly intelligent.

Itching hiney. After flossing, a spray of dental debris clung to the mirror. He was stabbed fourteen times, but luckily it was in the same place. What we have here is time, lots of time. Tribe Eyes Poker. William Graham Sumner's bootstraps seem large. The spread of mayonnaise was linked to the butter knife. Post-mortem sperm exists. Sometimes the little bunnies make it across the road. The sugar often thought it was salt. In the etiquette guide, Ed could find nothing on sucking marrow.

The lollygag reflex. The kinky garden hose bothered Andy. The air filter proved useless on

Mars. While beating a Tibetan monk, Chun-fai's beeper went off. When asked what tough love really was, Mr. Kincaid giggled. After her third C-section, Jane's time in the fifty-meter butterfly decreased noticeably. Out of cream, Nan improvised with a few drops of rich breast milk. The monkeys threw shit at the glass because they cared. Twelve trains later.

"Help is on the way" is not ideal. Ungodly amounts of cream. Jesus likes Santa. More seasoned firefighters consider fried pork skins a delicacy. There was just too much suntan lotion in the meat loaf. Scrotal edema: the unseen epidemic. If you must kill, kill yourself first.

Due to its nature, the umbilical cord is a good conductor of electricity. Organic peanut butter smears frighten the elderly. Kneecap pancakes. The old house held many possibilities, including bankruptcy. "I know what my woman needs." Craving the smell of prison, Terry killed a policeman. Ghandi was an Indian giver. The veins in her legs looked like strings of grape jelly. If you make bombs, it's best to use them and then make more. The hysterectomy upstaged the tonsillectomy. She fingered her rapist in the lineup. The old *TV Guide* seemed as useful as the new *TV Guide*. On learning of his positive HIV test, Frank thanked God from whom all blessings flow.

He was convinced that she deserved it and that he was the one to do it. The focal point of his idea needed glasses. One of the Siamese twins liked Hegel, the other did not. Stained glass eye. Those cookies, although golden and crispy, were made by hands connected to a heart filled with hate. The hairiest part of her body remains to be seen. Rattlesnakes are one way to make church less boring. The ersatz coffee was close, but no cigar. Slow down, I just got off the toilet.

Coated with lip balm, Ramone's lips burned faster than the rest of his body. Dolly meet Dali. The jelly between my toes is free. The dead and the dying have a lot in common. The fourth graders followed their teacher single-file to the classroom, as if everything was okay. No one. I repeat no one. No one.

Little Joseph

could always count on finding a bit of cheese beneath his mother's large breast. The darkest, loneliest corner of the planet is filled with people. Would you care for lemon in your tea? Two times two equals four o'clock. The most reliable thing about Thelonius was the blinking light on his VCR. No one seemed to care that mom pared her fingernails in the rice pudding. The way to a man's heart is through his chest. I accepted the poems only after glimpsing the revolver.

If you go to the trouble of concealing a weapon, it might as well be a really big one. Hot coffee screams. That gaggle of geese right there. Automatic days off include the prolapsed rectum. Never make eye contact with anyone pumping gas. Hiccups during a spit shine. Murderous Rage 101 proved to be a popular course. Having only one tooth, Cletus hung his head when offered a piece of gum. The weathervane on Libby's head only added to her sense of information overload. There's a bitter line between a lot of things. Having emphysema, Carl's SCUBA tanks were quite large. Of course you can believe it. The hungry wolf will stop at nothing, become confused, wonder why it has done so. Tweedle Dee enjoyed working at Circle K.

Her raised eyebrows indicated not surprise, but rather that the fishbone would not go down. The typical cardiologist may be described as persnickety. The machete proved once and for all that beauty is only skin deep. The burning tire necklace is technically not jewelry. That syrup bottle has really big breasts. The calligrapher shuddered at the thought of his wife's new bouffant hairdo.

If I weren't sick I'd be okay. Easy access to stupidity. After breaking his wing, the angel was shot. A thickened toenail padded with proud flesh. That man trembles because the newspaper slandered his wife. The public eye is just that. Plumbers stick together. I was dressed to the nines and then I wasn't. Her Dick Tracey was better than his Dick Tracey. The end is nearly. All day long the people of Toledo repeat the name of their city. Deep in the sun's nuclear oven, there is a phone that never rings. That history of Wales was 900 pages too long. A private drowning is best. Smothered with onions versus covered with cheese. During the siege of Stalingrad, many things sold as biscuits. Aqua Net versus Consort or vice versa. The average karaoke microphone harbors billions of infectious bacteria, some of which eat flesh. The rotten yellow toenail peels back to reveal a stringy tangle of bloody fibrous muck. Breakfast is the least important meal of the day. The food pyramids of Egypt draw mostly flies. From the mouths of babes we have yellow vomit. Don't let your job kill you. From five feet away, I felt the shiny green fly pound the clear glass. It's not okay to wash clothes before 8 a.m.

Primarily, more than anything else, church is boring. What the house lacked in charm, it made up in mortgage. Most, but not all, economic development leaders speak with a gravelly voice and drive red sport utility vehicles. On inserting a foot-long steel canula into a corpse's jugular vein and watching the dark blood pour into a glass jar, Pearl had a habit of saying in a rather not-nice way, "Ha, ha, ha." I might have been spell-checking or buying cat food as the F-5 tornado swept the plains of Oklahoma killing twelve.

Is a hallelujah chorus ever really necessary? Over 2,500 words to find and circle! That magazine seemed slick, and it was. Her long, thick thumbnail disconcerted me. The fat boy with the violin said his name was Drew. Out of OJ. The crab cakes in Baltimore are probably very good. I like the coroner because he always answers his pager. Older model air conditioners are impossibly heavy. The black phone rings much as the white. If you ever make your grandmother cry, you'll remember it at her funeral.

Those brain tumors seemed out of place next to the grape juice. I was relieved when she pulled a large rotting cod from her vagina. The slant of the weave in my jeans seems planned, more so than I'm used to. If you want to drill for water in El Salvador, then you probably need a vacation anyway. Like snakes, we shed our skin, but slowly, bit by bit, dust almost.

The pollywoggle

strikes the uninitiated as being impossible. What we need here are more Mormons. The dating service for mildly retarded people proved successful, so much so, that elderly couples, banking on their luck to have such natural caretakers, began complaining, crying that their sons and daughters needed not love, but peace and quiet, at home, with them, at least until they died. "Jesus, he's a swell fuck" is considered coarse, in terms of language. The grease under his nails indicated that he worked on scars.

Not that he knew how, just that he did. When separating the wheat from the chaff, be sure you know which is which. That biblical story is a boldfaced lie or something else. This font is called curly-q. Mustard on my sheets. Mayonnaise on my carburetor. Let me take this Kotex from my bleeding hemorrhoids and throw it in the street. Tear the wings from a butterfly, and you will slowly die. It's Waffle House that perpetuates the myth of flat bacon. That particular school board meeting was boring and uninformative. The rye bread was a bit ornery and prone to hyperbole, not to mention good for sandwiches. To watch a man starve to death requires patience. Slowly tearing a nail into the quick. Compared to life on Mars, life on Earth is closer. Each day is different, I am told. Coconut milk is sperm.

Prior to dispatching Gigi with a shovel, Gordon bought a shovel. Getting nailed in the back of a '57 Chevy may or may not be fun. Can't we just get a log? The unintended death came as quite a surprise. Jesus Christ Mary Mother of God, so on and so forth. People with third-degree burns are not gracious and have few kind words, especially when the bandages pull. I am so tired, I could eat a balloon. I killed a bug with a spoon. It made a sound.

The new millennium irritates me. Peter tried to scan the horizon, but it was too big. If at first you don't fall down, try again. I've got myself coming, and Bubble's too. Where have the riots gone? I've been told Hemingway was a writer, I've seen his books for instance, even read most of them, yet I've never met Hemingway, seen his grave or even one of his pencils. As the 747 hit the ground, Jane was embarrassed to find a tag still attached to her new slacks. The pig as sour grapes. The size of the chip on his shoulder impressed everyone. The bean in my eye does not bother me. The skinless man always complained.

The boiled egg has little to say. The non-dairy product coffee creamer passes through the body unmolested. The Crimean War was colorful. The serial stalker's orientation video provided his victims with much needed information. A green cap hanging on a brass doorknob. Cats won't know until you tell them. Bright eyed and bushy tailed is dangerous. Baby powder comes from babies. If one disease does not suit you, then another will. That newspaper headline is not obscure, too honest even. Chewing gum readily absorbs dirt. Cherokee Indians eating in silence at Kentucky Fried Chicken. Bumblebees in my popcorn. Short pants make the postman seem accessible, almost human.

The dick in his mouth is from last night. Disappointment rings. A hardboiled egg, floating in fresh urine. Why is it? Always. I could if I wanted to, but I don't. The cells comprising the lining of the mouth constantly shed, are swallowed, creating a condition of spontaneous autocannibalism. The scattering of hard pimples on her face was offset by a thin smear of frosted lipstick. The bird that sings at night, may not live to see the morning. My right foot is fundamentally different from my left. Covered with cold sores, Ben swam alone in the pool. Up one side and damn the other. It's really business as usual, these dead men on the lawn. The Kleenex soaked with lotion is too much. That Bessie bug is a real doozy.

The shortage of shopping-cart wheel repairmen is often blamed on the Japanese. The unidentified rind provided endless opportunities for personal growth. Uh, affix the stamp where you said a minute ago, right? The harvest of juicy pulp from beneath Edgar's scabs delighted everyone, including an old neighbor that most everyone thought was dead. The ripple in the toilet told me that someone had just been here. The knob said hot but it wasn't. Too many children—too many violins. If you are nude and stand perfectly still, a level of ash, waste, hair, and tears, accumulating in pyramid fashion, will eventually reach your chin. God has diarrhea, twice a week. Placating someone is often the

first step toward murder. It is often important
to distinguish between the living and the dead.
Her veins were filled with ice water, and that's
why she was cold. The person who lives and
dies by the sword probably owns one. Ordinary yellow teeth signals a lack of exposure to
modern culture, especially TV. Drowning is bad
enough. At least we die once and I know that
much and water head baby. Chicken tenders are
a sign of progress. A cucumber salad fell into
the ocean raising the tide at the Bay of Fundy
a quarter-inch more than usual. I tried to hang
myself and the rope broke. I tried to shoot myself and the rope broke. I tried to cut my throat
and the rope broke.

I was towing my grandfather's truck with
a rope when it broke. Glass powder in my tea
swirls but will not dissolve. I have an idea of
why but am not sure. Fingernail clippers work
on nerves as well. The wind is whipping the
green out of them bushes. The mayor told us
about a new mall and then he resigned.

I went home

and ate nougat. Certain colors will make you an Indian. I can't show you the blood clot in my head, you'll just have to take my word on it.

His titty tasted sour, like it needed a good washin'. Unsolicited phone calls, during dinner, are, in fact, a blessing. What you got here is about 90 percent hope and 10 percent something else. The crystal doorknob on the towel closet fooled no one. Sheetrock in the spin cycle. The dead singer said hello, hello, over and over. I took out her glass eye and made love to her head.

Unless there's a mass conspiracy (and there might be). Purloined cat food. I'm going to call my grandmother now and see if she's still crying. She looks at the label to see how best to dry the shirt. The cat could see the wind and liked to eat grass, too. The butterscotch pudding, well received at the wedding reception, only hours earlier concealed a small shipment of opium from Burma. Secretly Victoria longed for the load of cast iron pipe to tumble from the diesel flatbed and crush her like a bug. Talus and scree will not soften a fall. A newspaper, costing fifty cents, laid in the floor will remain there unless it moves or is moved. One hundred percent of accidents that occur in the home, occur there. Shut up and fuck me some more, but not so hard, she said, feeling for her teeth.

Although five pages were missing from the journal, the study of Pat's life could best be characterized as a yawning dog. I think part of the reason that I've been having these loosey-goosey stools is that everything has been so exciting. We've got to go now. He lacks verbal skills but he is a very good painter. He has trouble expressing that. So, he paints instead. The cat got fatter and fatter and fatter and then it was a dog.

Prozac—because Zoloft is for pussies. He was a nervous man, highly intelligent, recently returned from Glasgow with a pocket full of thumbtacks. The wisteria grew as I cut it, defying my obsession to kill the awful weed. The obersturmfuhrer had few friends. When I saw my name on the marquee I thought there must be some mistake, and there was. The fashion, it seems, for writers living in New Orleans, is to weave tales of vampires, which, if you've been there, makes perfect sense. Leave me alone and let me wipe myself. I won an award. I imagine my guts are moist. Did you lock up? Are the pansies okay for another night? Okay, I'll leave you alone. Tensile strength matters. Blood is ordinary.

With rapid phone refill, Hank kept his prescription for Luvox up to date. Being a fan of *The Bell Jar* is hard. Period. There is ri in there. Geese. Tossed to him in an arc, tossed to him in an arc, tossed to him in an arc. Jesus wiped.

Overweight, alone, bleeding to death from the nose. Belly full of roundworms, difficulty with the sit-ups. The gangly man ran the performance art piece like a machine, like a clean machine, like the people were sand. My friends in the nuthouse get their mail just like you and me. The weekend shelf project spanned twenty years. The foreleg of a roach, feathered, broken, lying on the hot plate of the Mr. Coffee.

Aunt Jemima comes onto my pancakes. A bit of granite gravel in the white of the eye. Got a salty chancre itching in my windpipe. Shipyard welding, a break from, the routine, unless, you're a, shipyard, welder. Dinner plate nipples whored for gum and beer. Toilet liquid soap dispenser empty, giving nothing, caring even less. The sickness unto death sounds as bad as it really is. Old man laughs at the young boy. It may be a while before he dies. I've been trapped in this sewer for days with nothing to eat but rat pills and fried shrimp that fall through the grate. Love lifted me, really really high. I was surprised to see that the penknife refused to flush, much as the fat-laden stool. I got heartburn in my stomach. I got mediocre rhythm. I got my mind set on fucking. Some days I feel like I fell from a tree. Some days I actually do. A good diesel turban will last a good long time.

Cat litter tucked between my toes. Strapping on the 2,000-pound bullet, looking for a good time. The preacher gave himself allergy shots in his thigh. We understand house payments and dental bills. It's winter. It's supposed to be cold. A mole, writing a letter, drops his pen, can't find it. Corduroy skin. For Christ's sake, pass the vinegar sauce. Poetry is a hole with a pair of pants sewn around it. We put our money together and it was the same. A stack of 'zines is a stack of 'zines. The founder and chairman wrote a users guide, which was insulting to the average user.

A bit of mold makes it seem like food. A busload of three year olds going to the Post Office. On the buffet, the fried corn balls are best. It was a sort of sweetish sickness. Dour and ribald. The modem squawks as if dying. I like my new desk. It has a hard surface that resists my pen. Never follow directions when alone. He could really improvise on the guitar but could not play. I have to go to work now. I didn't clean her up and that was good. It sounds cozy, being on the train trestle and all. Nature's way of saying things is tricky at best. I got a scab right over a major artery. Good has two syllables. You can pee in a jelly jar; you can do whatever you like.

The blinking curser. The ski planes couldn't land because of the snow. It's six degrees in Talkeetna. Her pregnant belly itched; something smelled to high heaven; it was a painful birth; the insurance was no good. The shoe store's national headquarters was in Nashville, over a thousand feet from a school zone, only two blocks from a church which was white and something of an eyesore since it had burned. Polar bear on fire, nothing making sense.

Electronic banking is dangerous. Always low on paste. I have to shoot the mistletoe from the oak tree. Now I have a reason to buy a gun. A single entry ledger is not useful for more than one entry. Ohhh, a porch swing. I hear a train in the distance. That's where it is. I played football professionally until I learned the loopholes. That's when things really started rolling. If I'm crazy over you what ever will become of the girl with the lazy eye? I bet I'm ovulating. Slowly peeling my nail to the quick. The old bitch just refused to say no. A drill bit in a bag of screws. The extension cord is more of the same. The sap ran and ran and ran and then quit. Soap in your eye. Try as I may try as I might. Cat's in the cradle with the baby. Jerusalem is always just over the hill. The Bigfoot researcher, or cryptozoologist, whichever you prefer, claimed to be Apache and had a leak in his roof. I got this Malamud short story on my desk. However many bullets there were didn't matter since it was the first one that killed her. The Hardy Boys on scroll never did take off. A total of four chocolate mints in the floor. Read this on the bus as well. The poster announcing his retirement was a joke. Them eyes in the back of your head. Got to where ain't nothing taste good no more. Coughing on the stool. Where's the love? The buffet featured food shaped like shit. My ribs done broke. Forget the tip, she just started yesterday. My in box and my out box are similar. Where's that damned canned spinach? Trust me on this one baby. Tempest tossed me a biscuit. Toothless in a tube top. The space on the paper is about like this, this, this... Got a little mole on my tummy next to a gaping wound sustained in a knife fight with a homeless man who fell from a train. The truth is, no one knows.

Hermaphrodites are scarce, but I seem to know them all. The people in hell. What the children of the world need today is clove chewing gum. I don't understand. If you move away, the goldfish pond will evaporate. I like to wake up slowly and think of nothing. When I run, a

dampness collects in my underwear. All wom-
en (and men) adore Diet Pepsi. I have to buy a
ladder. Shredded cabbage versus a thirty-year
mortgage. The armadillo is a sonnet or a ron-
del or some such thing. I'm the only one who
wonders why I take Prozac. Whenever Jesus
farted, the people flocked to his buttocks. I'm
beginning to think. Cooling gelatin too fast. The
crease in her forehead tended to collect beard
particles as well as tiny beads of mercury. He
had the look of a opossum in heat, greasy, nervous, unsure. "Fan blade with leading edge coated in cat hair" failed to yield search results. The
sebaceous cyst, under great pressure, between
thumb and forefinger, came to a head, hesitated,
then shot a lively stream of oily goo onto the
side of the tub where it dried and became a part
of things. Snatches of speech through pursed
lips. On the gravy train looking for a napkin.

The Feldenkrais practitioner

had dry hands. Virtual reality in the form of dough. The placenta made a slapping sound. Soft and easy to use. Itch my but. Swallow hard. Wrap pipe in back yard. A date is made of numbers, sometimes letters, sometimes both. If a coffee mug says world's greatest grandma, is it true? Inert clay is still polyvinylchloride. The worms in my brain are always hungry. Watch out. I'm getting ready for work. Crossing the River Jordan means a lot. Many countries end with Stan. Pack your bags and go, before I change my shirt. The fever swept through the town like a toy. Stating the obvious. Drilling the impervious. Scanning the photograph. Writing a poem. The lamp matches my desk on the bus. In a far away place there are far away people who know only that they are there, far away. Suddenly she looks at me anxiously. Writing for a newspaper, eating cheese, writing about cheese, fudging the time sheet.

The living dead are hard to distinguish. The metal blinds prevented us from seeing the family burn inside the mobile home. Rhyming with q. Say guano. I got squirrels in my bed. Everybody is porn. Travel alone and fast and be ready to pay. That is a washing machine. It's four minutes past the hour. That's a good trick. The school board suspended the juveniles without hesitation or the color gray. The cats pissed in the vent every nine days. Hard to say. It's on the tip. Granny you're like a little raccoon. I was very grateful that she had pulled the creeping rug back to its original location preventing a permanent curl in the leading edge of that beast. It's twelve days until January 9. The starving Eskimo woman hung her children, one by one.

The test of literature, panty hose, is whether or not one runs with it. Walking on thin ice, Jesus yawned. Trained to kill, Dagmar became bored with death turning her hands instead to pottery. Once bitten, and twice shy, Frieda declined a ride on the bread wagon. Chewing the razor blade, Ted saw his folly, tasted his blood.

I am comfortable in torn shorts, except in Japan. The hawk's feather protruding from the parking meter strengthened my conviction that land is not a commodity, but rather a kind of dumpling, better boiled than fried. Little vertebrae in the canned salmon, easy to crush and tasty with its thin film of spinal goo. A solid punch to the kidney, following a railroad spike through the right orbit, must be delivered quickly as the body falls lifeless rather suddenly. A retirement plan for muons.

Dismemberment brings dismay. The Christ figure knot. Did you set the alarm? Using the tapeworm to measure pain. I ate seventeen hotdogs, vomited fifteen, and shit two. Scarred by a propeller, the angry dolphin grew teeth, became a shark.

Tipping cows begins at home. Screened-in Portugal. He crushed the puppy's head with his hand. Then tried to pet the mother. An intensely watered lawn. The poison ivy made sores on my body. Sometimes what seems best is gneiss or corn. Pus rags, two for a dollar. One more scab

and the jar will be full. He denied killing the
puppies, but offered to pay for them anyway. It
takes at least three small boys to hold a mattress
down in the back of a pick-up going 70 down
the highway. In other words, two are not enough.
She choked on a mote. Television keychain.
Born without a head, the baby failed to thrive.
His record seemed spotless until he turned it
over. Most Bible verses will fit on a T-shirt. My
pipe went out. John's thick sputum slowed the
tornado perceptibly. Step on me real hard right
here. The pipe cleaner got stuck in his pee hole.
The stockbroker explained five ways to lose my
money.

Sandra pulled out a long knife at the Tup-
perware party, causing it to end before the ice
cream. After his leg was blown off, PFC Wilson
toyed with his hamstring until medics arrived.
Phlegm-producing foods hold some hope for
treating menopause. Incredibly, Dirk detected a
hint of apathy from the Kinko's clerk. For better
traction, Scott's South Pole expedition relied on
the liberal use of cat litter. I am not out to create
a normative mood. Those red velvet nipples
seemed alive with possibilities. In regard to the
dispute over the grocery bill, there seemed to be
some issue regarding the price of food items.

The stool was as difficult as it appeared it
would be. An early loan payment seemed un-
necessary. Oatmeal fails to disguise the sweet
taste of brains. There is cat hair in my human
genome. Evidently IBM thinks technology
is worthwhile. The grease fire started on his
head, spread to his armpits, then his groin,
finally erupting into an unstoppable inferno as

it crossed the short grassy knoll to his caked
and matted ass. I got your disease right here,
in a thermos along with my pet cricket. We'll
call him Sobriquet. Some things should not be
weighed, such as human flesh and justice.

Again flooded with the spearmint pleasure
of nonprogress. The difference between what it
takes and what it took. The coroner was speech-
less, raising questions concerning his ability
to speak and therefore conduct conversations
with the dead. It is common practice, it seems,
to ask for it. Until I got my tattoo, I was insane.
Buttered toasts. Instead of potato soup, we had
potato eye soup. A stack of fingers. Plugging the
toilet runs in the family. As a young farm lad,
Timmy often would shout at the summer calves,
"Pull that teat! Harder! Harder!" The rice boiled
over on the stove, leaving a sticky, foamy resi-
due. I know when my breath is bad. Reading on
the toilet is fundamental. Mark blamed his out-
rageous essay, "God Fucking," on a feral pencil.
It was either design Christmas cards or choke
on mop strings. The unwanted dog felt free. If
you can't beat 'em, hang around until you can.

The 2,000-degree sparkler is less dangerous
than the 1,500-degree sparkler. After boiling and
peeling, John's arm looked bad.

Everything takes up space. The control
group of the depression clinical trial was
apathetic, sometimes angry, at the carefree,
seemingly blissful attitude of the study group.
Creative non-fiction is more widespread than
thought. Last week corporate America did
pretty much nothing. I'm not convinced that the
people of Flynt, Michigan, really want to make

shoes.

Well, elections are around the corner and babies born without forebrains are too. Destroy old art, make room for even older art. A partially drowned man, lying flat of his back, can projectile vomit the contents of his stomach, usually beef stew, a good six feet straight into the air. The weak link in literature these days are your big book chains. Deadlines and integrity don't mix when there's space to fill. Instead of a penis, Jack has a lemon. In other words he has to squat and squeeze the urine from his lemon, much like making lemonade, except in Jack's case it's urine. When the roll is called up yonder, catch as catch can. I got your boudoir right here with your brisket and peduncles. Dirty fingernails are proof of the existence of dirt.

Putting time in a bottle is possible but you pretty much have to make it a full-time job. An airbag may or may not deploy. Eastern savings time sounds like a good deal. She had queer notions of love, which included wrapping fish and pulling horn hairs. I make a motion with my hand that we stand up on our legs and walk away. Where did all these books come from? Daniel Boone's brother knocked up Daniel's wife. Daniel didn't care because he had a raccoon hat. Berber carpet, with its checkered history, is not for everyone. Whiskbroom closet full of cream. I spend a fair amount of time following behind you finishing things you don't finish. Well, it's true! It's like her humanity flows right out with the clotted menses. I got a fax modem. I can throw my clothes in the floor. Be a good sport and lose. In the grip of tornadic winds,

a floppy disk is nothing less than a buzz saw.
Here, let me douse your joy with a splash of cold
pee. I'm not going to bed yet. Earplugs, I used to
have a bunch you know.

Products such as Pussy Cream and Omnip-
oop keep this country on top. Apparently the
federal government is sick. What I wouldn't
give for a riding lawnmower: a flooded copper
mine. Scratch and win sounds fun. A skull is for
holding brains and drinking soup. The camera
in my bladder doesn't work anymore. Scratch
me here before I combust. I use different battle
cries, depending on how much pain I'm in.

Topsoil has taken over our Earth. Keeping
the fresh towels in the root cellar did not work
out as planned. Besides being far from the
bathrooms, the towels began to sprout. Cheese
overload is an individual process. The spoon-
fork seemed to vanish beneath the twenty tons
of avalanching snow. Instead of a nametag, use
a Q-tip dipped in caramel, then candy sprinkles.
When the dentist told me to close my eyes, I
did. The method of congestive heart failure is
to choke the lungs with fluid. As a social climb-
er, blue ropes cover a wide variety of settings
including cocktail parties and visits to the psy-
chiatrist. By attaching my Weimaraner calendar
to the bottom of my Camaro, I don't know what
day it is. The *chkk chkk chkk* lawn sprinkler versus what? You get your bus routes mixed up and
you're liable to regret it, especially during hard
times. The asexual bag boy asked for my driver's
license. As church pianist, the sandpaper on the
piano keys made Celia feel better.

There are too many mountains to climb, not

enough people to fall off. I am told that this beer
is indeed "Genuine." Beneath her tight white
sweater, I imagined her breasts were raw. The
old man, an apparent "victim" of "Alzheimer's
disease," slept with his legs in the air and soiled
himself continuously as if "unconscious" of his
actions. Everybody that I know is struggling
with it. Sporkalicious, down to the last whin-
ny. Outside, dusk drew a curtain over Singing
Springs and some kid drew a bird in China.
Can't you not do that? Can't you not understand? What's not wrong with you? Mohammed
declined the aperitif, noting that he did not
shave. I feared the Rangers knew these woods
better than I. Life in the Outer Hebrides, according to *People Magazine*, consists of late night
fun and wool. The last train to London will be
crowded. After nine years in the Sahara, Dean
was able to formulate an image of the desert.
His image, when drawn, appeared as a bright
sun beating down on golden sand. Not unique
by any means, but clear. Let your diagnosis
work for you not against you. Frank's night-
mares of death ended upon waking. The FBI has
a hand in most everything, including the fancy
furniture industry. Pass the mung beans, please.
Anyone for more Artane? The ticket said admit
one so I told about the time I burned down the
barn.

Acne

vulgaris. A solid conducts sound more efficiently than baby food. I noticed he had a part in *Hello Dolly*. Then I ate a pretzel. When I shave my head, people can see the sores. I write for a small newspaper. My fingers hurt all the time. I've got more blood in my little finger than all of the telephone books in Stalingrad. The catfish nuggets remained undigested in Audrey's gut for a good week. If I wake up and see Satan at the foot of my bed one more time, that will make seven times.

Stacked like cordwood, the corpses presented little threat. Thrown like a banana, the knife merely squished on Amanda's neck. Portly little fucker just wouldn't sink. I generally run until some sort of structural failure renders me helpless. The ribs did not need barbecue sauce. They were my ribs and I was alive.

Having been taught by his mother that the brain was a single yellow wire, Ned failed medical school. If your right hand offends you, talk to somebody about it. Having died and gone to Hell, Bad Apple Adams pretty much had it made. No animals, no friends really. Paste and knobs everywhere. Pain pills as a substitute for salad. During a mudslide, mud will slide. My knee has fluid on it. I will probably be okay. The calendar year hates the fiscal year. Out of an early dislike for others, I absorbed my twin in utero. The highway was strewn with heavy metal guitars. Jack London beat his dogs.

Hey Freddy, drop your nutsack in the coffee for a sec' will ya'? After a life of force-feeding ducks, Jacque was diagnosed with arthritis. It's no fun to expect an eclipse. One of the von Trappe girls married a Stubbs. It's possible to hang yourself with your own intestines. In the midst of war, cookies are a welcome break. Anyone can throw pottery. Forgetting she was pregnant, Jenna huffed paint thinner on the roller coaster. Instead of a Down's baby, Hope gave birth to a UPS delivery man.

The Liberty Bell is cracked for a reason. The surge protector looked silly lying on the beach. Left for dead, I had few qualms.

Carpets on display

apparently for sale. Here comes Todd. She doesn't know if her 305, poetry for fools, is gonna make this fall. The comforter is on sideways. Hooray! I found my little bottles (brother). They put some of their mail with my mail. The entire toenail. Grit in my derailleur. It's a great cooler. There is a ruckus below decks. Any reason these shorts are in the floor? At the daycare they seemed excited by the prospect of new infant openings. I'll let you hold the little lamb. Try our new skillet. Choose from five brightness settings.

I became a sexy beast for the good of others. She needs to pull outta here by nine. Gel. Pass the glioma. Investigatory. Part of the equation is how you feel about it. Grandpa got mad if we flushed the toilet paper. Scrap iron pancakes. Antiperspirant=Alzheimers. Endless pecan-tree-related activities.

Which poofy handkerchief, this one? We'll always live here.

Monkey grass crowds the azalea. Legitimate brick. Gar scales used as arrowheads. It's where the pee comes out. A couple extra more. Dante's Impala. Shoddily applied sunblock. Minivan sheathed in wonton skin. Burned astraddle familiarity. The valve salesman reluctantly took his vacation. Steamboat Annie? Your order is ready. Banker slash poet. The earth ends everywhere. Troublesome time toilet. I keep thinking it's enough. Grammar crutch. Dissatisfied with the sock drawer. The D-ring broke, then he drowned. Each year the music festival becomes less interesting. No, Elsa. He said we couldn't afford it and that made it special. My foot will look better after I soak it in Clorox. You've never been choked, that's the problem. Her safe zone was between Marguerite's thighs. He didn't mind the box wine because that's the kind he buys.

If you see a dead or dying animal, don't touch it, just tell the ranger. Flash cameras disorient the baby turtles. The butter, a pot, and his shoes. The size of the paper may affect what Larry writes. Thimbles, one cubic meter, in a wheelbarrow. How can that be, sting? The blind man throws his crutch away, only to discover that he is blind. You need trash. What's your name in Indian? Not the sauce I ordered. Prone to corn silk.

Viable as well as adequate. Hey there lonesome, want some more asparagus? That country has funny boundaries and stuff. Reverend Cockstroker. Drive-up meme window. I'm holding my spine and something is wrong. Say it isn't fresh. Cerumen? Epistaxis? Marijuana cigarette? Fairly beholden and whatnot. It's all that crazy stuff you've been reading. Due to lumbago, I've cancelled my trip to Sheshamane. People in their clown suits, working. The laser printer hums. I really can't stomach this inequity of shelving. Tiny cobwebs cling to paint dimples. A book on two-stepping without a barcode. Uncognizant. I bit Ray. Sticky goat food.

Anita Bryant

likes pie. Pretty big thumb lunula. Never-
mind, ever again. The German lady told me
to hurry away from the rabbit cage. Beaten
senseless until the Raisinets appear. Forgive me
Father, for I am not known for what I have done.
Here we are, looking death in the eye. Baby
coughs like dog barks. Overwhelmed with wisteria. If a bottle of water costs three dollars, it's no
longer a festival. Funny credit history. My camp-
ing methods drove him mad. George Plimpton
told a funny story. Harper Lee inspects an apple.

We have unlimited weekend minutes, but
there are only 2,880. How big is your fever?
Before unloading, vent the limestone slurry.
She touched the hem of my shorts and began
to bleed from her eyes. Mutually assured flux.
I had one sip of beer and felt full. Yakking with
the neighbors. A fool and his funny bone. The
sound we make when the cows are late. If you
smell your pee, drink a glass of water. Torn cuticle salad. Proud and willing flesh. The bone and
couch man.

Henry kissed integers, plotted to kill my
father. The flyswatter crushes and smears. I
dropped a frog in the well and cried. The pipes
were old and predated the use of toilet paper.
Cats among the broken weathered boards. Feeling punky, whoopsidaisical. Cerulean cerumen.
I popped an eye. The BB gun wasn't very strong.
Buying rugs, giving them away. I wish I could
draw, and I can.

We vented her body. Do's and fonts. Baby sleeps, then wakes up. My cell phone is sporty and blue. John Denver flew paper airplanes. White gas. I had to excuse myself because I wanted to ride my bike. Well, I haven't showered today. Kidney-shaped figs, food for the towhee. Personalized chicken. Foramen ovale envy. New York City is littered with Starbucks. A dead jelly-fish, just the head. My own personal Shibboleth.

Vanilla cream Tums. Can I have an "Omen?" I got charged for thirty-two feet, sixteen feet too many. My top three rocking chair colors. He knew a lot about the murder scene. The aisle was closed, keeping the lattice-board out of my reach. Two bad apple days in a row. This pencil writes upside down. Just let the old cast-iron tub drop into the basement and leave it there. Organ paste. Do the innkeepers make fresh cookies every day? Croatinine. Three blackberry thorns pierced my left thumb, hit the bone. The sewer beneath the interstate was filled with boulders. I had to hurry back and order pizza. Tired of guessing, I fell asleep. She put her mascara on "by the spoonful." After twelve years in college, Georgette married, moved to Augusta, and joined the country club. It was his game leg. I gave the monkeygrass a haircut. I tickled her with the red pencil. Ancient Mayan ruin. The dead ponies delayed closure. Christian software. The sowbug sleeps on the zinnia. We made ourselves have fun on Memorial Day. The ribs are frozen solid. The water in the baby pool is cold. She pulled weeds; I fixed the fence. To get your way, play the part. I didn't know the names

of the flowers, except the common ones. I went
mushroom hunting once, when I was alone.

There is a band-aid stuck to the mirror,
which requires explanation. The breaker can't
handle the load. She failed to realize she was fat.
I can hear the wasp's head collapse. Sine qua
non crayon. The United States is a coral reef. My
friend Dick Brains. I hope they find Mallory's
camera. Well, instead of surgery, why not try
a thicker pad? Those charges are trumped up.
Feet of cake. He fell into the job as he would a
crevasse. The hormones in meat and milk will
sprout pubic hairs on girls as young as eight. It
occurred to me that I could save the hummus
and eat it later.

Sometimes websites are out of date. A seal
of approval, a penguin of shame. The mocking-
bird would not die. Gambling, before or after the
buffet? One percent of his body wasn't burned. I
took out the garbage and grass stuck to my feet.
Hairball on the comforter. Backpack pressure
points. Just a bit further father. Creamy white
footstool. Don't let guns go to your head.

If grease is food,

I'd say we ate well. Paralyzed by the spider's poison, the firefly could only blink. The maps had different streets on them. If I break my leg, I'll call you. Are those cat knees? The blower motor for the '97 Civic is $59.95. Well there's always blue. I had to work really hard today. The trip was a flop. My backpack strap broke and I became angry, then defeated, then happy.

They lived in the campground pretending that they arrived yesterday. First, they tacked Jesus to the cross and he fell off. Taking her first steps, she staggers as if on fire. Tarantula in the bandanas. A bowl of Cheerios is equivalent to four ounces of imitation crab meat. Destroyed by a tornado, the card shop was disorganized. Keno makes us better people. Mistaking the chevron for a rainbow, Scotty penetrated the vapor barrier. The roach lived, but not for a reason. Alphabetical list of friends. I am crawling to meet you. Over the dishwasher, the plane sounded like a violin. It's pretty, but we never use it. I feel like it's garbage day. Is it my imagination or is that real? Lesbians can live a long time. Baby thinks grated Parmesan cheese comes from the giant's beard. Plasmapheresis is a business with accounts payable, etc.

A barrel of pencil shavings soaked in goat semen. According to *Harper's*, the Pope used to catch big air. The rejection was well written, informative, and kind of like a tumbleweed. Did you notice I washed the combs? Cracks between

the fingers, reddened with yeast. The skin is a
slow kidney. I believe Preduzece is a type of rifle, or a font. The pen clicks, the pencil does not.
Warning! Blastocytes. As the helicopter flew
over, all thoughts turned to Gunter Grass, then
an airplane flew over, and all thoughts turned to
brewers yeast. It's been four years since I tasted shrimp and grits, far too long if you ask the
shrimp.

Baby enjoys the milder cheeses. Write this
book. She was punctual during a period of ques-
tioning and long o's. I think it was the day I cut
my thumb with the tape gun. I peeled the dried
skin from my side and wrote on it a fetching
tale about a packet of lost zinnia seeds. The test
burn at the new chemical weapons incinerator
went really, really well. Too tired to read, I just
looked at the words. My lens fell into the salad.
Let's ban schools of thought and stick with what
works. The battery exploded but still held a
charge. She got her start at a truck stop. Brack-
ish water equivalent of Lydia. 44:58, 44:59, 45:01.
I felt like a bull with a broken leg, being driven
to the butcher, beaten with a club as I hobbled
on three legs.

We are four miles from the steak house.
Sect leaders have fun. What's it like living in
the Congo these days? Now that I know I'm
dead. In the letter, she told about how much
she enjoyed learning about Jesus. I'm having
vertical thoughts, or at least what appear to be
partitions, perhaps, between my thoughts, thin
ones. Marketing somehow fanagled research
into foamy plasma. I took a shower because the

sheets were clean. Are you having fun yet? The
meatloaf is half brains. If I were God, I'd make
the armadillo's head bigger. John is made from
maple leaves.

Check your pockets for kleenex. Note to
self: buy maggots. She coughed and took off
her glasses. I will not be de-frocked. Racing's
triple crown. High-heeled storm pit. Free books
are hard to read. Remodeling leads to divorce.
Anxiously awaiting the hook's appearance. She
paints drowned women. Encountering the Great
Wall of China, the Mongol warrior went in and
had the buffet. Take the train and be done with
it. I have to give everybody a little something.
The orchid was told to die. A vocabulary of thirty words including: apple, Petey, and zap. That
degree is not useful. Scabies et veritas.

Dirty French poodle. The pattern in the
carpet speaks to me: "Do not pay the bills."
There was a large fire near my house, about
three blocks away, so I went down there. Excited
about the plane tickets. Unclear, injured thumb
x 2. We talked about poetry and I told the day-
care story. Her ex-boyfriend noticed little heads
as well. She said she feels sticky "down there."
Malted conjunctiva.

Edamame, Edam, Ed, and me. Instead of
throwing the caul away. Chiggers is bad news.
Check in, check out—hotels are complicated.
Hard, hard banana. Scrambled egg messages,
received over and easy. Barrel scraping. Mus-
solini, Mao, and Macy's. We were told that
her surgery lasted 1 point 5 hours. There were
lots of good vibes and multitudes of nefarious

plenipotentiaries as well. Right smart. Buttermilkograph. Thin canvas shoes, green, a size too small, and always wet. A momentary flap of rhizome. Monumentally perpendicular. It's not the worms that glow, but the larvae.

Let me fight you. Camel cricket skin graft. Not sullen, but carefree like a man with no friends. Let me see your pen. Several times a day, I can't take it anymore. My brother's name is apple pie and he is yet to be born. For an ounce you get 1/16th of a canto. Wayne Newton steals chickens. Grape leaves stuffed with leprosy. Readers chew. Crewel pants. Infuse your hair with vitamins. The hamburger buns are too soft. Amtrak's not doing well. I pledge allegiance to the Gulf of Mexico. A moth wants in. Bone chip 'neath the kneecap. Keep your Cadillac, give me your Clark's. Clam dipped in talc. Eyes clot the pipe. I-beam X-ray. Fleshy, heavy. She missed carrying her baby. Infected harelip. One girl holds puppy's head, one girl vomits.

I take my cake on a napkin. Nice crapper. Cat looks mad. I came and ran fast. Herring smoked over dung, sprinkled with peyote. The crack in my skull no longer weeps. A sight exclusively for sore eyes.

She did not shave her legs and then became barren. He played nice some of the time. She mentioned a cup of Joe several times. Did you check (pee) on her? On the Fourth of July, Halloween, and New Year's Eve, people are mean. Hyperreflexia does a body good. She reads the Bible with her foot.

Crib slats. A strong suit of gum tools. Instead of sex, let's write letters. I've never had anyone take this long. Eight points of light. Milk preparedness survey. Praise the word and pass the linguist. From now on I will fix it all. Ice pencil. Funds off balance. Roy Orbison's carapace. Sylvan intestinal flora. That's his best coffee grin. Tadpole gelatine. "Eggs!" cried father. "My eyebrows are eggs!" World Wars come. Powder tamper and father of five. Shot through the heart, Vick was tempted to point fingers. Thumb lips. Saddle block–enhanced soda. Manni was supposed to wait. Forget trains, I'm talking paperclips. Finnish page. The fifth dementia. Will you help me real fast? The trains are never late at the hippy school. Turn your suicide around with Mucomist!

Aminophylline handshake. I know why the birdcage squeaks. When I was eight, I wanted to break my arm. Wallet fat with maps. I will pray for the youth mission trip. That's the kind of shit you deal with. Mental health avocado.

Her mother, who was killed when she was eight, didn't die right away. Heavy iron stares. She just up and went to Ireland. Little debit cakes. Open DNA connectivity. Complimentary wheat grass juice and then what? Let's pretend that I sell you my soul. There are thirty-six kinds of people. Please God, help me first. Beautiful people with thrip heads.

Everything was cool

until Wanda Jackson accepted Christ as
her personal gravy. No, you take your shoes off.
Elba and Sylacauga. Cuticle splicing device,
Pat Boone pending. Ancient alpine-pesto runes.
Pleh is on the yaw. Ted scented candle. I had
trouble benefitting. After six months in the rock
polisher, Justin felt smooth. Square dance death
camp. Ear lobe kernel epidemic. Do not best me.
Wasp nest heart valve. Train your child in the
ways of cement. Farafaraway. Jars of unopened
cedillas. Neighbor's dog makes a rocket. Wag-
es with sage and mayonnaise. $299 + tax, $30
rebate on core. Out of stock everywhere.

My heart, does not break, but tears, regularly.
One flat per week. Practicing idiot. Dear Patient,
your insurance rots and we hate you. It's a cheap
ticket and I'm on edge. Tincture this, a methio-
late sky.

Instead of sperm, Olaf produced spores. Lost
dog's chain clacks on pavement. Nature's big
bag. Phone book seeks order. Another broken
back, another trend. 700 butterfly profiles.
Uncanny day-care triangle. Count your blisters
while I poop. Candy ass problems. You affront
me. Maternity leaf. I didn't realize that it didn't
make sense. Going off, kind of rambling. Execu-
trix. Cat's brass sensibility.

All of Freddy's shows must go on. Guar gum,
even in the popsicle. Herman is a good name.
A/C kicks in, lights dim briefly. Blue laundry
basket, beige laundry basket. Hold the pen,

press it down, move it around. Early morning
airport air. Yucky daycare, halls filled with frogs.
Long green grapes like toes. 12 x 12 = 144 tran-
quilizers. Children's TV is tripe with virtue. The
heated lines of gold melt into the tortoise shell.
I've momentarily lost center. What we have here
are bolts. We turned her on to natural childbirth.
Play with fire, go on, play with it. Inside the clear
baggie I could see a cracker, a pay cut, and a
bit of cheese. My mama loud. Scrap iron book.
Today was small.

Bar talk vaccine. Bridging the gamut. Skin
sticks to leather couch. Lusty teen chooses sex
over Sunday School. I started smoking when I
lit the cigarette. Proust lived in a hot attic eating
prunes and drawing hats. Velvet Kelvin. Theory
of scant genetics. I can scarcely fear you. Con-
tinue to drive or do CPR? Buffet items swim.
Well Toby, the ink just stays in the skin. Apple
stem, stem cell, cell block, fungo bat. Sunrise
over the trampoline, dew on the slide. She full
and cut her lip. Dirty cwm. Neither the black
girl nor the white girl could lift the mule. Chipo
broko.

I'm tired, fan belt. Back against the story.
Tiny camera in my heart takes pictures, makes
a clicking sound, causes clots. An unnoticed
wink. Chicken farmer selection process, phase
two: the interview. Brace your shelf. Cold pillow.
Nouns and plasmids. Erstwhile crack. *Carmex,*
the movie. Maybe I gottem at Jenny's house.
Corporeal murmur. Cat on the sweat pants. He
thought friends were watching the baby. Weirs,
fish, and otherwise, as well as waterhammer. The

end of a done day. Red grapes in wet paper towel. Ask God for a dollar. Shouldna done it. Bad
words make us small. Hinged buttocks, brass.
Boil your pens. Human seismograph. Spate of
clips. Read fescue. Stay home, read Bible, grow
long, straight hair, drown children. Teacher
nixes book review idea, gets breast cancer. Right
up there with nobody. Underneath is the red.
Warm cakes of dandruff. Here comes a fluffy
bunny, and there's a radio! There is one Negro
in Oregon.

Oh, what a wonderful e-mail! Decline of the
able-bodied greeter. Carefully hidden among
the potatoes. Hot pear. Tooth strikes sink. My
child is pretty. Is that your thatch? U.S.S. *Pajama
Bottom.* Ectopic fantasy. Cat refuses to swallow
hair, dies young. Save all Teds. The birthday party across the street functions without us, apparently without any weird or ill effects. Catheter
stopped up. Talking pork rhizomes. The crazed
pee. Errorotomy. Show daddy how you march.
A springbok in every crockpot. Black and white
people. Bug-eyed Jesus. The B&B's green lawn
piled high with heads of horse.

Popsie's uncooked egg. Pale impish incest,
battleship gray. Fluent melanoma. Mellifluous
conjunctiva. Let me weigh your breath. I took a
test. The bug man came. I'll feel better tomor-
row. Brown n' serve dinner fools. Beetle stuck to
baby's shoe. Creaking okra. Stone cracking. The
parts affected are your hand, foot, and mouth.
Until change. Amniotic paint thinner. Look
mole. Prize regression. Red ferns. Fractal stim-
ulus. We'll have to cough it up and get a breast

pump. Chez situation. We cut our hand. Animosity to facilitate the break. An eyebrow, funded. Be brave and force the child to write letters, long letters. Old man fucks stove. My changing bowl. She feeds intuit.

The ways of snow and bone. Off your Koestler. Ink/lotion. Fat you use. Cable snaps, bend knees. Put out with sex. Riparian foam. Interstate of adduction; a singing horse, four lanes, no median. Sequential flyer miles. Turtle lays eggs in garden. Bird pins snake on thorn. Devil eats turtle eggs. Quarter pounder with fleas. Liquefaction vs. cremation. Minnows within garlic distance.

Sauercat. Adit, a letter, the Hebrew, number 23. Paper tray is empty. Cardiovascular intensive care, brown shag carpet. Jesus's mittens ruined. Info desk, a box of biscuits. Especially hard were her bones, which sang much as Samson's pillars. For emphasis, Tonya outlined her scarlet letter with feces. Dressed to kill, Rodney killed Amy, who, as luck would have it, was dressed to die. Stanch it mister. Train howls in the basement. "Help me! My head is being ripped from my body.........—rrrrrrriiiippp!: "Aaaaahhh!!" !=0. 47.

www.ingramcontent.com/pod-product-compliance
Lightning Source LLC
Chambersburg PA
CBHW032044180726
48284CB00008B/2739